SPACE

PLANETS FAR FROM EARTH

IAN GRAHAM

W
FRANKLIN WATTS
LONDON•SYDNEY

An Appleseed Editions book

Franklin Watts
First published in Great Britain in 2016
by The Watts Publishing Group

Designed by Guy Callaby
Edited by Mary-Jane Wilkins

Picture acknowledgements
t = top, b = bottom, l = left, r = right
title page Aleksandar Vozarevic;
2-3 CoreyFord; 4-5 Dimitar Marinov/
all Thinkstock; 5b NASA, ESA, H. Weaver
(JHUAPL), A. Stern (SwRI), and the HST
Pluto Companion Search Team;
6 CVADRAT; 7 Sabino Parente; 8 Stephen
Girimont; 9 patrimonio designs ltd;
10-11 Elenarts/all Shutterstock; 12 Digital
Vision/Thinkstock; 13 FomaA/Shutterstock;
14 Ablestock.com/Thinkstock; 15 Byron
W.Moore/Shutterstock; 16 Lars Lentz;
17 Jason Reed/both Thinkstock; 18 JULIAN
BAUM/SCIENCE PHOTO LIBRARY;
19 Stocktrek Images; 20 Elenarts;
21 Stocktrek Images/all Thinkstock
Cover tl MarcelClemens/Shutterstock;
tr Digital Vision; br MarcelC; bl Martin
Adams/all Thinkstock

Every attempt has been made to clear
copyright. Should there be any inadvertent
omission please apply to the publisher
for rectification.

Dewey number 523.4
HB ISBN 978 1 4451 4916 5

Printed in China

MIX
Paper from
responsible sources
FSC® C104740

Franklin Watts
An imprint of
Hachette Children's Group
Part of The Watts Publishing Group
Carmelite House
50 Victoria Embankment
London EC4Y 0DZ

An Hachette UK Company
www.hachette.co.uk

www.franklinwatts.co.uk

CONTENTS

THE FAR PLANETS

Eight planets travel round the Sun.
The four closest to the Sun are small worlds.
The four furthest from the Sun are giant planets.

GAS GIANTS

The four planets furthest from the Sun are sometimes
called gas giants because they have no solid surface, no land.
Instead, they are made mostly of liquid and gas.

Jupiter

MANY MOONS

The far planets have lots of moons. Jupiter has the most, with more than 65. All four of the far planets have more than 160 moons altogether.

SPOTLIGHT ON SPACE

The gas giants are cold worlds because they are so far from the Sun.

Saturn

Uranus

Neptune

THE NINTH PLANET

Until 2006, there was a ninth planet. It was a tiny planet called Pluto. But when more worlds like Pluto were found, astronomers decided to call these small worlds dwarf planets.

JUPITER

If you see a really bright star in the sky at night, it might not be a star at all. It might be the giant planet Jupiter.

MIGHTY JUPITER

Jupiter is the fifth planet from the Sun and the biggest of all the solar system planets. It's so big that more than 1,300 Earths would fit inside it.

Jupiter's stormy atmosphere is divided into light and dark bands.

GREAT RED SPOT

Lots of storms race around Jupiter. The biggest is called the Great Red Spot. It was seen for the first time more than 300 years ago and it's still there today!

WHAT'S IT MADE OF?

Jupiter is made mostly of hydrogen with some helium and other gases. Under Jupiter's clouds, the gas is squashed so hard that it changes into a liquid.

SPOTLIGHT ON SPACE

The Great Red Spot is a vast storm bigger than Earth.

EXPLORING JUPITER

In 1610, Italian astronomer Galileo Galilei looked at Jupiter through a telescope and discovered its four biggest moons. In recent years, Jupiter and its moons have been explored by space probes.

GALILEO

A spacecraft called *Galileo* spent eight years exploring Jupiter and its moons. It was the fifth spacecraft to visit Jupiter. The first four flew past Jupiter. *Galileo* was the first to orbit it.

Galileo went into orbit around Jupiter on 8 December 1995.

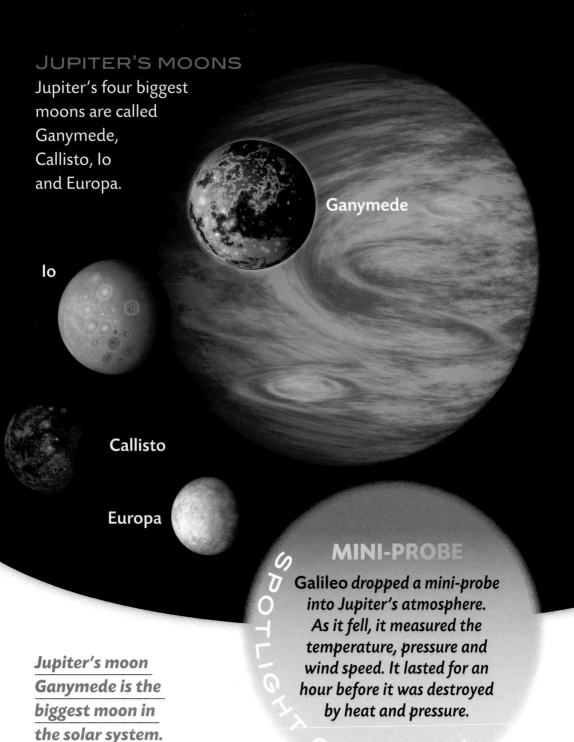

JUPITER'S MOONS

Jupiter's four biggest moons are called Ganymede, Callisto, Io and Europa.

Ganymede

Io

Callisto

Europa

Jupiter's moon Ganymede is the biggest moon in the solar system.

MINI-PROBE

Galileo dropped a mini-probe into Jupiter's atmosphere. As it fell, it measured the temperature, pressure and wind speed. It lasted for an hour before it was destroyed by heat and pressure.

SPOTLIGHT ON SPACE

9

SATURN

Saturn is a beautiful golden planet surrounded by broad bright rings. Like Jupiter, it looks like a bright star in the night sky.

A DISTANT GIANT

Saturn is not quite as big as Jupiter, but it's still a giant planet. It's made of the same gases as Jupiter; mostly hydrogen with some helium.

Saturn takes 29 Earth years to travel round the Sun.

SATURN'S WEATHER

Saturn is ten times further from the Sun than Earth, so it's a very cold world. It's also very windy. Winds blow around Saturn at more than 1,600 km/h.

SPOTLIGHT ON SPACE

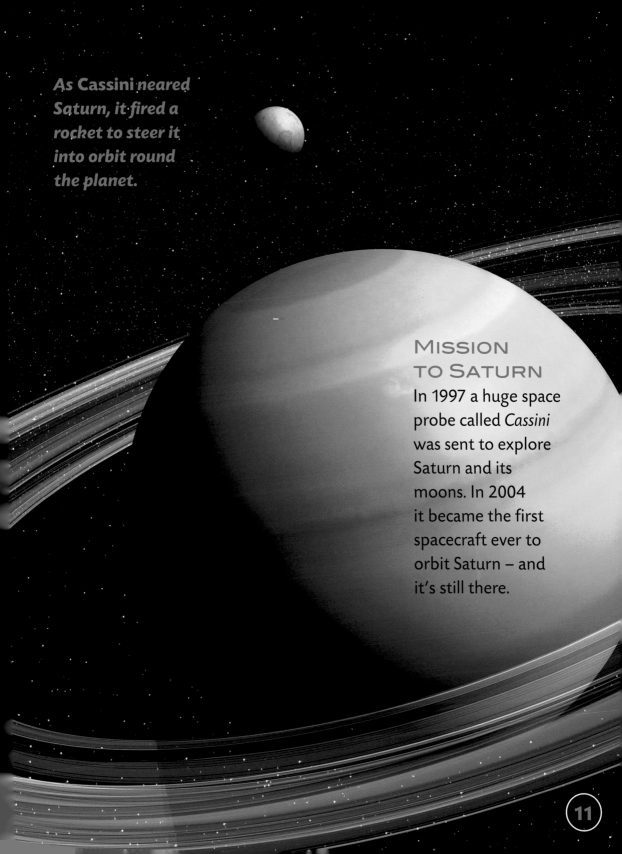

As Cassini neared
Saturn, it fired a
rocket to steer it
into orbit round
the planet.

MISSION TO SATURN

In 1997 a huge space
probe called *Cassini*
was sent to explore
Saturn and its
moons. In 2004
it became the first
spacecraft ever to
orbit Saturn – and
it's still there.

SATURN'S MOONS AND RINGS

Saturn travels through space with dozens of moons and the countless millions of tiny moonlets that make up its rings.

WHAT ARE THE RINGS MADE OF?

Saturn's rings are made of millions upon millions of pieces of ice with a little added rock. Some pieces are as small as specks of dust. Others are as big as buses.

Saturn's rings are so bright because they reflect sunlight like millions of mirrors.

By 2013, 62 moons had been discovered orbiting Saturn. More will probably be found.

NEW MOONS

When the *Cassini* space probe left Earth, Saturn was thought to have 18 moons. *Cassini* discovered many more. It also found more rings that are too faint to be seen from Earth.

LANDING ON TITAN

Cassini dropped a mini-probe called Huygens on to one of Saturn's moons, called Titan. Huygens found a strange, cold world with a thick orange atmosphere and lakes of liquid methane.

SPOTLIGHT ON SPACE

Uranus

Uranus is less than half the size of Jupiter and Saturn, but it's still a gas giant. More than 60 Earths would fit inside it.

Methane gas gives Uranus its blue-green colour.

A BLUE-GREEN WORLD

Uranus is made of the same gases as Jupiter and Saturn – hydrogen and helium – but it has more water, methane and ammonia.

ODD ORBIT

Uranus orbits the Sun in a very odd way. One of its poles faces the Sun for 42 years and then the other pole faces the Sun for the next 42 years.

Uranus is surrounded by 13 faint rings made of dark dusty particles.

TELESCOPE DISCOVERY

Uranus was the first planet discovered by using a telescope. The astronomer William Herschel discovered it in 1781. Other astronomers had seen it before, but didn't know it was a planet.

SPOTLIGHT ON SPACE

Neptune

Neptune is the smallest and most distant of the four gas giants. It orbits the Sun 30 times further away from it than Earth and was not discovered until 1846.

TWIN WORLD

Neptune is similar to Uranus. Methane in its atmosphere gives it a rich blue colour. Neptune has the fastest winds in the solar system, blowing at up to 2,400 km/h.

Neptune and Uranus are both very cold planets, at about -200°C.

ROGUE MOON

Neptune has 14 moons. Triton, its biggest moon, orbits Neptune in the opposite direction to the other moons. It probably formed elsewhere in the solar system and was then captured by Neptune.

GRAVITY TUG

Neptune was discovered by studying Uranus. Astronomers noticed that Uranus was being tugged by another planet's gravity. When they looked for the mystery planet, they found Neptune.

Neptune's biggest moon, Triton, has volcanoes that spew out nitrogen gas.

SPOTLIGHT ON SPACE

Saint Benedict
A Catholic Voluntary Academy
Duffield Road, Darley Abbey
Derby
DE22 1JD

GRAND TOUR

Every 175 years, the far planets line up in space. They move into the perfect positions for a space probe to fly past all of them.

SPACE VOYAGERS

In 1977, *Voyagers 1* and 2 were sent on a grand tour of the far planets. *Voyager 1* flew past Jupiter and Saturn. *Voyager 2* flew past all four of the far planets.

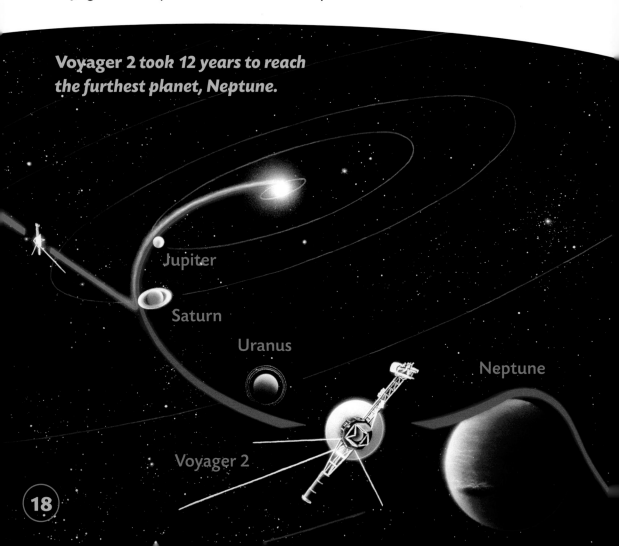

Voyager 2 took 12 years to reach the furthest planet, Neptune.

Jupiter

Saturn

Uranus

Neptune

Voyager 2

The Voyager space probes have a big radio dish to send information to Earth.

LEAVING HOME

In 2013, *Voyager 1* became the first man-made object to leave the solar system. *Voyager 2* will follow it. Their instruments will continue working and sending information to Earth until 2025.

HELLO FROM EARTH

In about 40,000 years, the Voyager *space probes will fly past stars. Just in case aliens ever find them, both spacecraft carry golden discs with sound recordings from Earth.*

SPOTLIGHT ON SPACE

DWARF PLANETS

Astronomers have found five small worlds they call dwarf planets. There could be thousands more waiting to be discovered beyond the far planets.

SMALL WORLDS

The five dwarf planets found so far are Pluto, Ceres, Eris, Haumea and Makemake. Most of them were found in part of the solar system called the Kuiper Belt.

The Dawn spacecraft on its way to dwarf planet Ceres (right) after visiting asteroid Vesta (left).

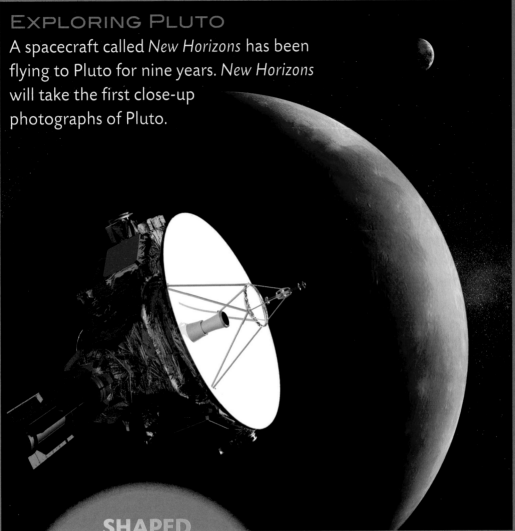

EXPLORING PLUTO

A spacecraft called *New Horizons* has been flying to Pluto for nine years. *New Horizons* will take the first close-up photographs of Pluto.

SHAPED BY GRAVITY

To be called a dwarf planet, an object must orbit the Sun and it must be big enough to be pulled into a round shape by its own gravity.

Five moons orbit Pluto. The biggest, Charon, is half the size of Pluto.

SPOTLIGHT ON SPACE

Saint Benedict
A Catholic Voluntary Academy
Duffield Road, Darley Abbey
Derby
DE22 1JD

GLOSSARY

ammonia A chemical substance containing nitrogen and hydrogen. It is found as a gas on Earth and in the atmospheres of gas giant planets.

astronomer A scientist who studies the Universe beyond Earth.

atmosphere The gases that surround a star, planet or moon.

dwarf planet An object smaller than a planet that orbits the Sun and is massive enough to be pulled into a round shape by its own gravity.

gas giant A large planet made mainly of gas and liquid.

gravity A force that pulls objects towards each other because of their mass.

helium The second lightest and second most abundant element in the Universe. Helium is found in stars, gas giant planets and, in small amounts, in Earth's atmosphere.

hydrogen The lightest and most abundant element in the Universe. Hydrogen powers stars such as the Sun. It's also found in gas giant planets.

Kuiper Belt Part of the solar system beyond the planets where scientists think there are millions of icy worlds, including dwarf planets.

methane A chemical substance containing carbon and hydrogen. Methane is found in a planet's atmosphere.

moon A small world that orbits another body such as a planet.

orbit The path of a planet, spacecraft or moon around a larger body.

radio dish A metal bowl that reflects radio waves, often used by spacecraft to send and receive radio signals.

ring Pieces of ice or dust forming a flat disc orbiting a planet. All four gas giant planets are encircled by rings.

solar system The Sun and all the planets, moons and other bodies that travel through space with it.

space probe An unmanned spacecraft sent from Earth to explore planets, moons and other bodies.

WEB SITES

http://solarsystem.nasa.gov/planets/profile.cfm?Object=Uranus
Lots of facts about Uranus from the American space agency NASA.

http://www.kids.nineplanets.org/uranus.htm
You can read about the strange blue-green world Uranus here.

http://www.ducksters.com/science/neptune .php
Find out how Neptune was discovered and how it compares with Earth.

http://factsforkids.net/neptune-facts-kids/
The top 30 facts about Neptune.

http://kidzone.ws/planets/jupiter.htm
Lots of facts about the giant planet Jupiter.

http://www.sciencekids.co.nz/sciencefacts/planets/jupiter.html
Even more facts about Jupiter.

http://www.esa.int/esaKIDSen/SEMJL6WJD1E_OurUniverse_0.html
Find out more about Saturn, its moons and rings from the European Space Agency.

INDEX

Saint Benedict
A Catholic Voluntary Academy
Duffield Road, Darley Abbey
Derby
DE22 1JD